# Look Out, Mouse!

by **Steve Björkman**

Holiday House / New York

Copyright © 2015 by Steve Björkman
All Rights Reserved
HOLIDAY HOUSE is registered in the U.S. Patent and Trademark Office.
Printed and Bound in October 2014 at Tien Wah Press, Johor Bahru, Johor, Malaysia.
The artwork was created with ink and watercolor.
www.holidayhouse.com
First Edition
1 3 5 7 9 10 8 6 4 2

Library of Congress Cataloging-in-Publication Data
Björkman, Steve, author, illustrator.
Look out, Mouse! / by Steve Björkman. — First edition.
pages cm. — (I like to read)
Summary: When Farmer Fred forgets to feed the horse,
the mouse helps out and later, when the mouse is
in trouble, the horse repays his kindness.
ISBN 978-0-8234-2953-0 (hardcover)
[1. Horses—Fiction. 2. Mice—Fiction.
3. Farm life—Fiction.
4. Helpfulness—Fiction.] I. Title.
PZ7.B528615Loo 2015
[E]—dc23
2014006416

ISBN 978-0-8234-3397-1 (paperback)

For Kacie
and Ethan

It is dinnertime on the farm.

But Farmer Fred forgot
to feed the horse!

The mouse
nibbles and
nibbles.

Look out, mouse!
Here comes
the cat!

Look out, mouse!
Here comes
the snake!

Look out, mouse!
Here comes the owl!

Look out, mouse!
Here comes
the weasel!

Look out!
The fox is
coming too!

Look out, mouse!

The horse
neighs.
The dog barks.
The chickens
cluck.

Farmer Fred wakes up.
"What is going on out here?"

It is dinnertime
for the mouse.
Look out, house!

# You will like these too!

*Come Back, Ben* by Ann Hassett and John Hassett
A *Kirkus Reviews* Best Book

*Dinosaurs Don't, Dinosaurs Do* by Steve Björkman
A Notable Social Studies Trade Book for Young People
An IRA/CBC Children's Choice

*Fish Had a Wish* by Michael Garland
A *Kirkus Reviews* Best Book
and Top 25 Children's Book

*The Fly Flew In* by David Catrow
An IRA/CBC Children's Choice
Maryland Blue Crab Young Reader Award Winner

*Late Nate in a Race* by Emily Arnold McCully
A Bank Street College Best Children's Book of the Year

*Look!* by Ted Lewin
Correll Book Award for Excellence
in Early Childhood Informational Text

*Mice on Ice* by Rebecca Emberley and Ed Emberley
A Bank Street College Best Children's Book of the Year
An IRA/CBC Children's Choice

*Pig Has a Plan* by Ethan Long
An IRA/CBC Children's Choice

*See Me Dig* by Paul Meisel
A *Kirkus Reviews* Best Book

*See Me Run* by Paul Meisel
A Theodor Seuss Geisel Award Honor Book
An ALA Notable Children's Book

*You Can Do It!* by Betsy Lewin
A Bank Street College Outstanding Children's Book

See more I Like to Read® books.
Go to www.holidayhouse.com/I-Like-to-Read/